# Whose Eyes Are These?
## A Look at Animal Eyes—Big, Round, and Narrow

Written by Peg Hall
Illustrated by Ken Landmark

Content Advisor: Julie Dunlap, Ph.D.
Reading Advisor: Lauren A. Liang, M.A.
Literacy Education, University of Minnesota
Minneapolis, Minnesota

Whose Is It?

PICTURE WINDOW BOOKS
Minneapolis, Minnesota

Editor: Lisa Morris Kee
Designer: Melissa Voda
Page production: The Design Lab
The illustrations in this book were prepared digitally.

Printed in the United States of America.
1 2 3 4 5 6 08 07 06 05 04 03

Library of Congress Cataloging-in-Publication Data
Hall, Peg.
  Whose eyes are these? : a look at animal eyes—big, round, and narrow/ written by
Peg Hall; illustrated by Ken Landmark.
    p. cm. – (Whose is it?)
  Summary: Examines a variety of animal eyes, noting how they look different and
function in different ways.
  ISBN 1-4048-0005-0 (lib. bdg. : alk. Paper)
  1.  Eye—Juvenile literature. [1. Eye. 2. Animals.]  I. Landmark, Ken, ill. II. Title.
  QL949 .H28 2003
  573.8'8—dc21        2002005778

Picture Window Books
5115 Excelsior Boulevard
Suite 232
Minneapolis, MN 55416
1-877-845-8392
www.picturewindowbooks.com

# Open your eyes and see who's who.

Look closely at an animal's eyes. Eyes can be big or small. Eyes can be close together or far apart.

Eyes can tell you how an animal finds food or how it stays safe from its enemies. Some eyes shine in the dark. Other eyes work like telescopes to make small things look bigger.

Eyes don't all look alike, because they don't all work alike.

Can you spy whose eyes are whose?

Look in the back for more fun facts about eyes.

Whose eye is this, watching for danger?

This is a zebra's eye.

The zebra has eyes on the sides of its head. This lets the zebra spot danger from both sides without turning to look.

Fun fact: A zebra's eyes are always alert. Even when the zebra lowers it head to eat or drink, it is still looking for signs of danger.

6

Whose eyes are these, looking for prey?

These are a tiger's eyes.

Like the eyes of many hunters, a tiger's eyes face forward. It is more important for the tiger to see the prey running in front of it than to look behind it for enemies.

Fun fact: Tiger eyes shine at night. Each eye has a special layer that acts like a mirror and makes moonlight bounce off of it. The special layer helps the tiger, a night hunter, see better in the dark.

Whose eyes are these that look so strange?

These are a housefly's eyes.

Like other insects, the fly has compound eyes. A compound eye is made of lots of tiny lenses joined together. Compound eyes help the fly see moving things in almost every direction at once. A fly can see your hand coming up behind it. That's why it's so hard to catch.

Fun fact: When a fly looks at something, it sees a fuzzy picture. The picture is made of lots of tiny pieces that fit together. Each piece comes from a different lens in the fly's eyes.

Whose eyes are these, poking out of the water?

11

These are a crocodile's eyes.

The eyes of a crocodile sit on the top of its head. The crocodile can hide underwater and hunt for food with only its eyes and nose showing.

Fun fact: Crocodiles shed tears, but that doesn't mean they feel sad. The tears in a crocodile's eyes wash and protect them.

Whose eyes are these, peeking out of the sand?

13

These are a ghost crab's eyes.

A ghost crab's eyes sit on stems. The crab hides in the sand with only its eyes sticking up. The eye stems bend and wave around, letting each eye look in a different direction.

Fun fact: A ghost crab has compound eyes just like a fly. Seeing things move above and behind it helps the crab catch its food.

14

Whose eye is this, never blinking?

This is a snake's eye.

A snake never blinks or closes its eyes, because it has no eyelids. Instead, the eyes are protected by clear covers, like built-in safety goggles.

Fun fact: The cover on a snake's eye comes off as the animal grows. When a snake sheds its skin, the eye cover comes off, too. A new eye cover takes the place of the old one.

Whose eye is this, staring from above?

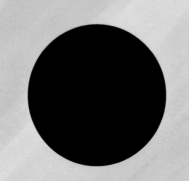

This is an eagle's eye.

An eagle's eyeballs are shaped like tubes. They work like telescopes and help the eagle see things that are very far away. Even when it is flying hundreds of feet above the ground, an eagle can see a tiny mouse far below.

Fun fact: An eagle's eyesight is about six times sharper than a person's. Eagles can see movement better, too. A running animal that looks like a blur to us is clear to an eagle.

Whose eyes are these, looking back at you?

These are your eyes!

Just like other animals, you use your eyes for finding things and for staying safe. Your eyes also tell others how you feel. Your eyes can look sad or angry or happy. They can wink with a joke or blink with surprise. Are your eyes ever sleepy? Do they ever snap shut?

Fun fact: The black middle parts of your eyes are your pupils. Pupils let light into your eyes. When it is dark, your pupils grow big and let in more light. When it is bright, the pupils get small and let in less light.

# Just for Fun

Whose eyes are whose?
Read the riddles and point to the answers.

I am a snake.

My eyes are always watching for danger. Who am I?

I am a zebra.

I can see your hand coming up behind me. Who am I?

I am an eagle.

My eyes shine in the dark. Who am I?

I am a tiger.

My eyes never blink. Who am I?

I am a fly.

My eyes work like telescopes. Who am I?

# Fun Facts About Eyes

**SEEING IN COLOR** Animals do not all see colors in the same way. Kangaroos cannot see different colors at all. Giraffes can see a few colors. Apes see the same number of colors that most people see. Many butterflies probably see even more colors than apes and people do.

**UNDERWATER EYES** Many animals that hunt underwater have eyes with very large pupils. That's because it can get dark in deep water, and large pupils let in more light.

**EYES THAT TURN** A chameleon's large eyes stick up and turn in all directions. With each eye moving in a different direction, the chameleon can see in almost all directions at once!

**DO RHINOS NEED GLASSES?** A rhinoceros does not see very well. Like some humans who wear glasses, the rhino is near sighted. That means it sees things that are near but has trouble seeing things that are far away.

**SEEING SPOTS** Worms and starfish have eyespots instead of eyeballs. Eyespots let these animals tell the difference between light and dark, but they can't see anything else.

**PUT A LID ON IT** Most birds have three eyelids. Like you, they have one eyelid on top and one on the bottom. Their extra eyelid moves sideways. That's the one they use to blink. Birds close their top and bottom lids only when they sleep.

# Words to Know

**compound eyes** Compound eyes are made up of lots of lenses. They are very good for seeing fast-moving things.

**lens** A lens is a clear part of the eye that covers the pupil. It helps you see objects clearly.

**prey** An animal that is hunted and eaten by another animal is prey.

**protect** To protect means to keep safe.

**pupil** The pupil is the black, middle part of the eye. It gets bigger or smaller to let light in or keep it out.

**shed** To shed means to get rid of. A snake sheds, or gets rid of, its skin.

**telescope** A telescope is a special tube that you hold up to your eye to make faraway things look closer.

# To Learn More

## AT THE LIBRARY

Fowler, Allan. *How Animals See Things.*
New York: Children's Press, 1998.

Franco, Betsy. *Why the Frog Has Big Eyes.*
San Diego: Harcourt, 2000.

Gordon, Sharon. *Seeing.* New York:
Children's Press, 2001.

Hartley, Karen, Chris MacRo, and Philip Taylor.
*Seeing in Living Things.* Chicago:
Heinemann Library, 2000.

## ON THE WEB

Lincoln Park Zoo
http://www.lpzoo.com
Explore the animals at the Lincoln Park Zoo.

San Diego Zoo
http://www.sandiegozoo.org
Learn about animals and their habitats.

Want to learn more about animal eyes?
Visit FACT HOUND at
http://www.facthound.com

# Index